ZELDA'S SECRET

PASCAL LEMAITRE

ZELDA'S SECRET

Troll Medallion

Zelda had a secret—a secret dream. She was afraid that if she told anyone, they might laugh at her. So she tried very hard to keep it to herself. But finally she just couldn't hold it in any longer.

"Nina, you're my best friend so I'm going to share a secret with you. Someday I'm going to be a prima ballerina. Now you won't tell anyone, will you?"

"Of course not," said Nina. "I'm your best friend."

Nina really did try to keep Zelda's secret.
But one day when she was talking to
Nono, the rhino, she just blurted it out.

"Now please don't tell anyone else," begged Nina.

"Of course not," said Nono. "A secret is a secret."

Later, while playing cards with the giraffe sisters, Lilli and Lulu, Nono tried to take their minds off winning by telling them Zelda's secret.

"Now please don't breathe a word of this to anyone," said Nono.

"Don't worry," they assured him. "Zelda's secret is safe with us."

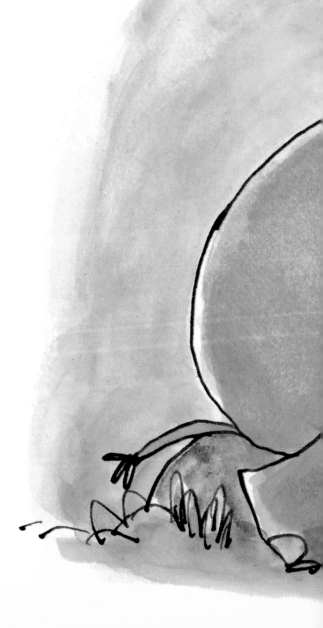

But Lilli and Lulu loved to gossip. Before long all the monkeys in the trees knew Zelda's secret.

"Now keep this to yourselves," Lilli and Lulu told them.

"Our lips are sealed," answered the monkeys.

In no time at all, even the parrots were telling Zelda's secret to anyone who would listen.

"We know Zelda's secret! We know Zelda's secret," they squawked.

When Zelda overheard them, she ran away and began to cry. Old Oliver, the wise owl, fluttered down to see what was the matter.

Zelda told Old Oliver what had happened. "I'll teach your chatterbox friends a lesson," promised Oliver. "Just wait until tomorrow."

Old Oliver was a bit of a magician. When night fell, he cast a spell with the help of the crescent moon.

Chatter, chatter,
Gossip and squawk.
Now see how easy
It is to talk!

In the morning, all of Zelda's chatterbox friends found themselves tongue-tied.

When Zelda saw them she laughed so hard she fell over and rolled on the ground.

But wise Old Oliver soon put a stop to that.
   "Zelda," he said, "it's not nice to laugh at other people's troubles. If you want to be a ballerina, it would be better for you to spend your time practicing."

Old Oliver quickly removed the spell. "We're sorry we didn't keep your secret," the animals told Zelda.

She forgave them, of course.

Months later, all the animals were in the audience when Zelda gave her first performance at the J.B.T., the Jungle Ballet Theater. Everyone was so proud to be her friend.

Zelda was so popular, she was invited to make an around-the-world tour. All her friends came to wish her luck. Zelda promised to send them postcards from every city she visited. Then the whistle blew, and it was time to leave.

"Bon voyage, Zelda!" everyone cheered. "We know you'll be a big star!"

Production and copyright © 1994 by Rainbow Grafics Intl.
Baronian Books S.C., Brussels, Belgium.

Published by Troll Associates, Inc.

First published in the United States by Bridgewater Books.

Printed in the United States of America.

10 9 8 7 6 5 4 3 2 1

Library of Congress Catalog-in-Publication Data

Lemaître, Pascal
Zelda's secret / by Pascal Lemaître
p.   cm

Summary:
When Zelda the elephant tells her best friend
about her secret dream, it isn't a secret anymore.

ISBN 0-8167-3309-0 (lib.)
ISBN 0-8167-3310-4 (pbk.)

[1. Secret–fiction 2. Jungle animals–Fiction.] I. Title.
PZ7.L53734Ze   1994
[E]–dc20   93-28448